BABY'S WORLD

a first picture catalog

photographs by Stephen Shott

Dutton Children's Books · New York

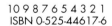

Copyright © 1990 Dorling Kindersley Limited, London

All rights reserved.

CIP data is available.

First published in the United States 1990 by
Dutton Children's Books
a division of Penguin Books USA Inc

Published simultaneously in Canada by
Fitzhenry & Whiteside Limited, Toronto

Originally published in Great Britain 1990 by
Dorling Kindersley Limited,
9 Henrietta Street, London WC2E 8PS

First American Edition   Printed in Italy

10 9 8 7 6 5 4 3 2 1
ISBN 0-525-44617-6

Additional photography by Stephen Oliver
(pages 34 - 35) and Dave King (pages 36 - 37)

Dorling Kindersley would like to thank:
Hamish Anderson, Roxanne Bance,
Christian Harman, Troy Hunter, Holly Jackman,
Rebecca Langton, Emily Morrison, Sam Priddy,
Kerra Stevens, and Aaron Wong for appearing
in the photographs in this book;
Boots the Chemist Limited and
Jacadi Limited for loaning props.

Contents

Me

bottom

back

head

hair

leg

knee

eyebrow

eye

cheek

nose

mouth

arm

arm

hand

ankle

hand

foot

toes

hand

fingers

thumb

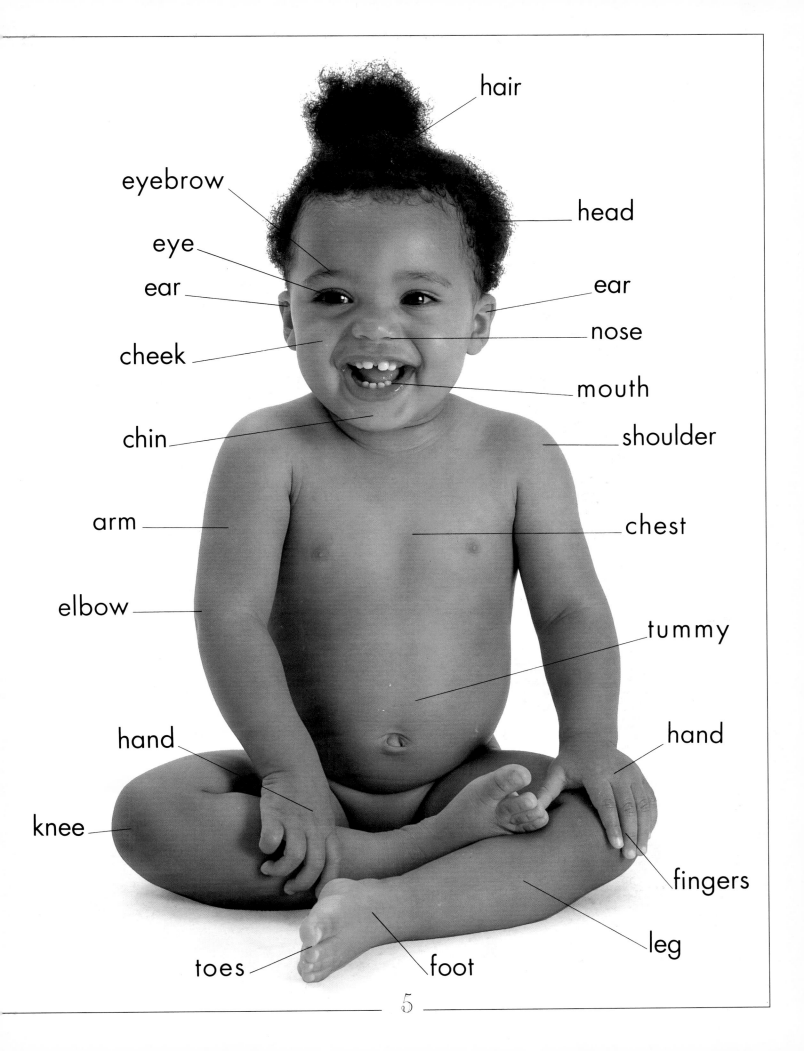

hair

eyebrow

head

eye

ear

ear

nose

cheek

mouth

chin

shoulder

arm

chest

elbow

tummy

hand

hand

knee

fingers

toes

foot

leg

5

In My Room

lamp

hanger

book

mobile

slippers

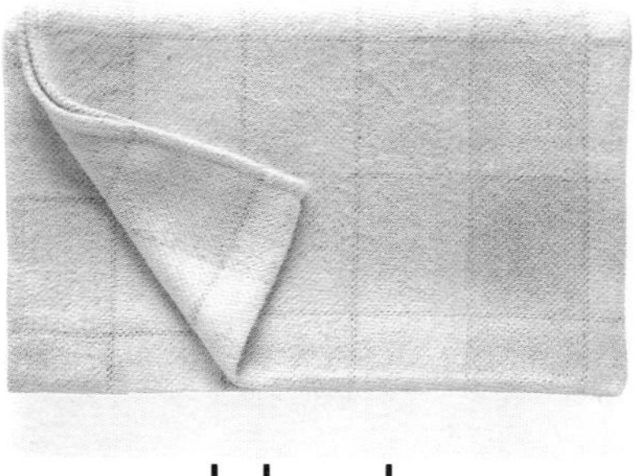

blanket

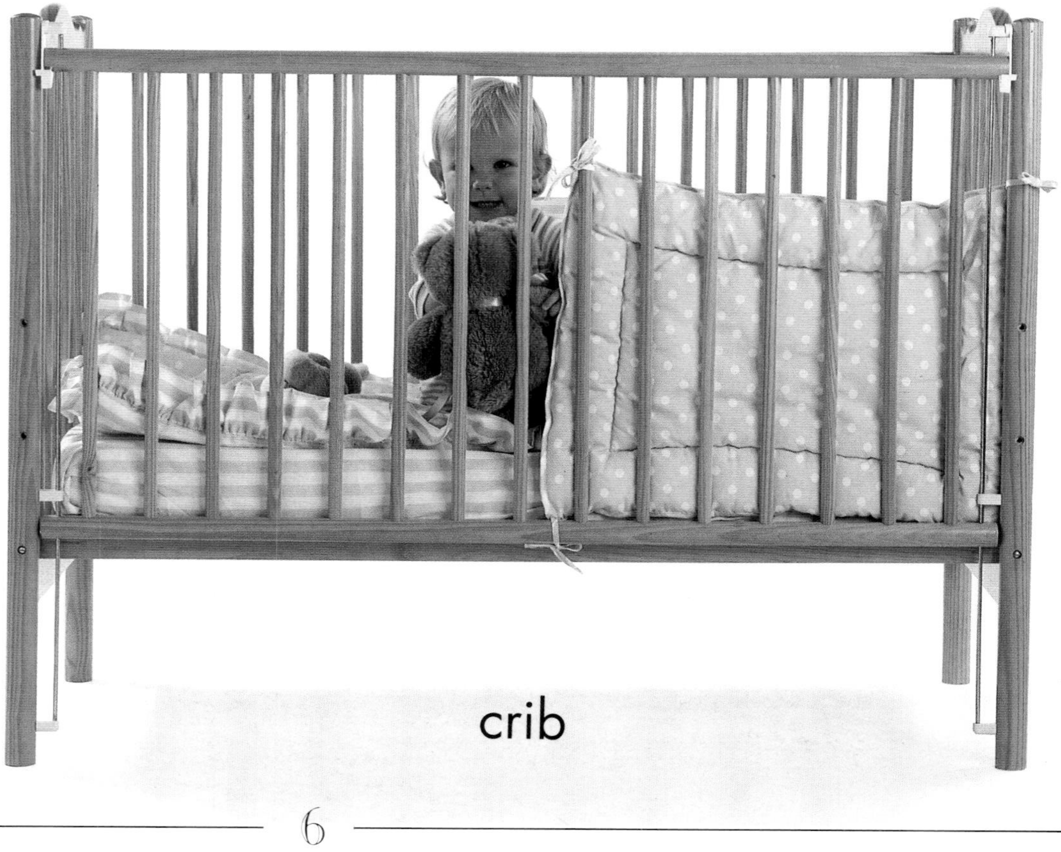

crib

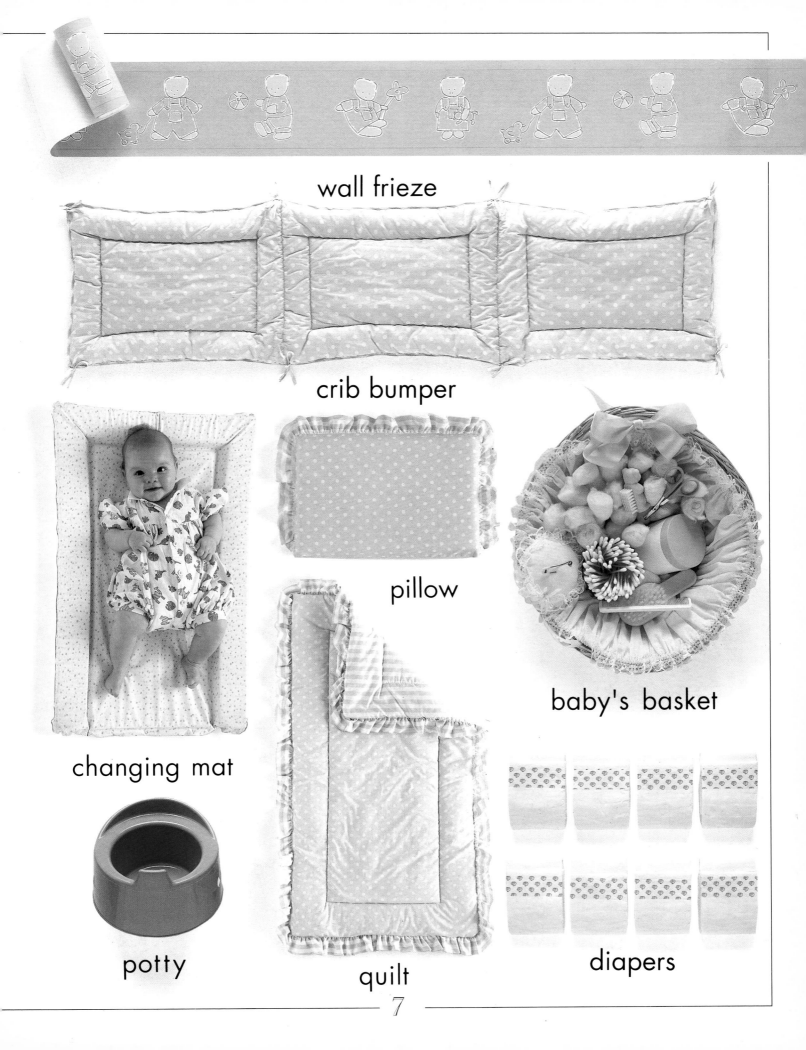

wall frieze

crib bumper

pillow

baby's basket

changing mat

potty

quilt

diapers

My Clothes

sun hats

playsuit

tee shirt

shorts

shirt

overalls

stretch suit

undershirt

underpants

socks

shoes

slippers

booties

shoes

sandals

warm hat

scarf

dress

jacket

trousers

mittens

sweater

socks

shoes

slippers

shoes

sneakers

rain boots

9

Getting Dressed

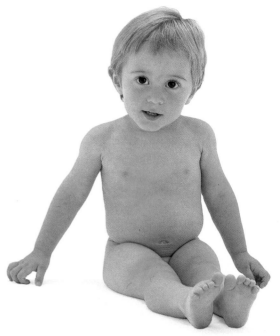

1. When baby wakes up,
he is wearing his sleep suit.

2. Now he has
nothing on.

6. Now baby
is in his overalls.

7. He pulls
on his socks.

8. Then he puts on his shoes.

5. And then his shirt.

3. His diaper is
   put on.

4. Then his undershirt.

9. He says "Good morning"
   to his teddy bears.

10. He is ready
    for breakfast.

Eating and Drinking

bottles

bibs

bowls

spoons

forks

cups

bibs

bowls

Mealtime

The babies are in their high chairs.

This baby is playing with his food.

This baby is drinking from a cup.

This baby is eating
a cookie.

This baby is drinking
from a bottle.

My Toys

doll

teddy bears

stacking toy

puzzle

activity center

soft blocks

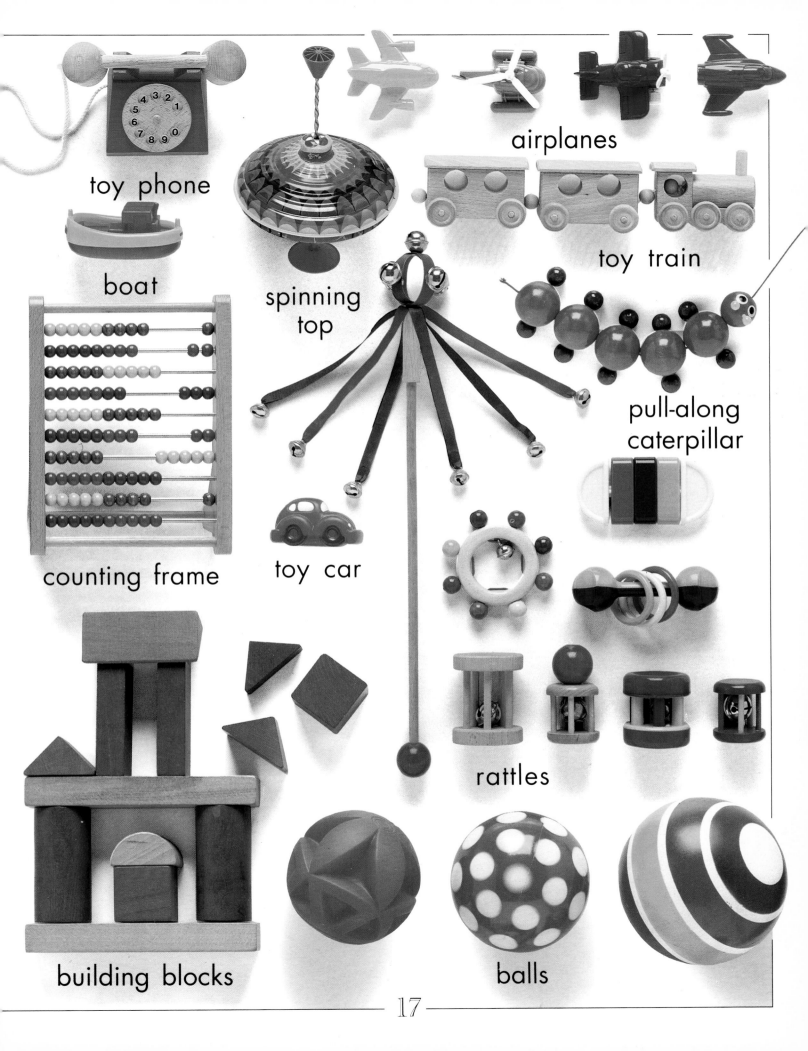

toy phone

airplanes

boat

toy train

spinning top

pull-along caterpillar

counting frame

toy car

rattles

building blocks

balls

17

Toys That Go

pull-along caterpillar

push-along duck

toy train

wagon

doll stroller

tricycle

wheelbarrow

Colors

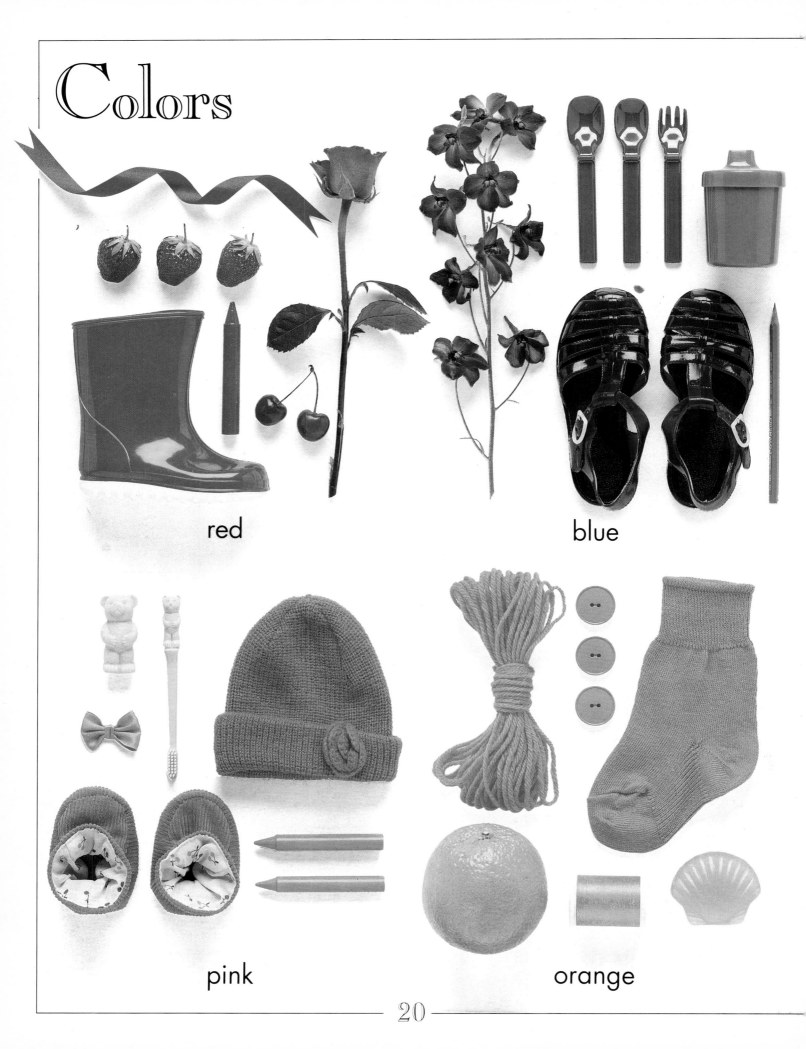

red

blue

pink

orange

yellow

green

purple

brown

Pets

kittens

goldfish

puppies

birds

rabbit

cat

Moving Around

kicking

sitting

lying down

crawling

playing

kneeling

crouching

getting up

walking

standing

25

Out and About

The babies are in their strollers,
ready for all kinds of weather.

Warm days

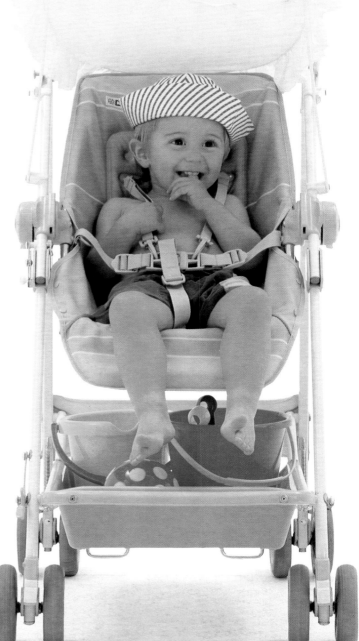

Hot days

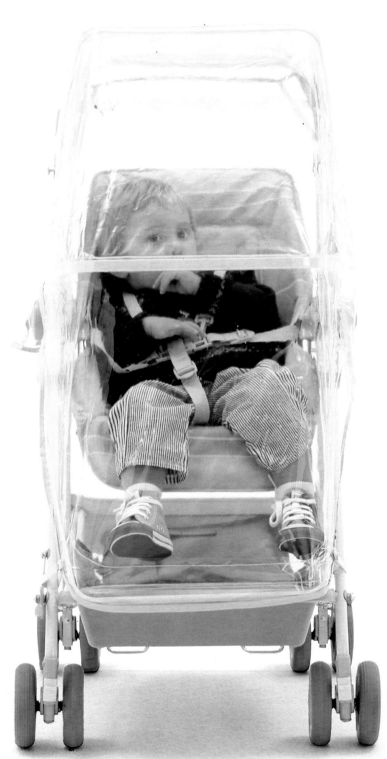

Wet days

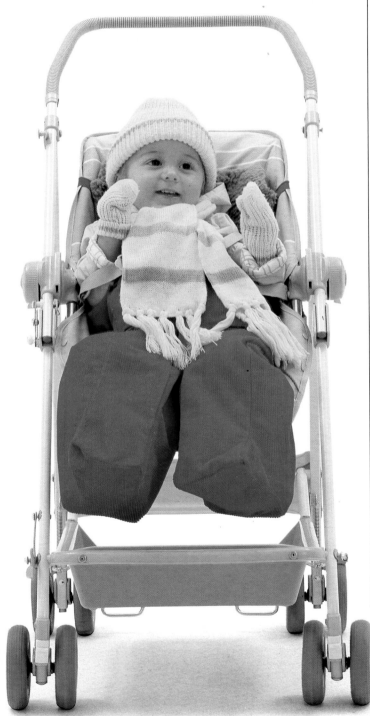

Cold days

Things to Eat

banana

cherries

peach

strawberries

orange

grapes

apple juice

apple

grape juice

tomato

yogurt

animal crackers

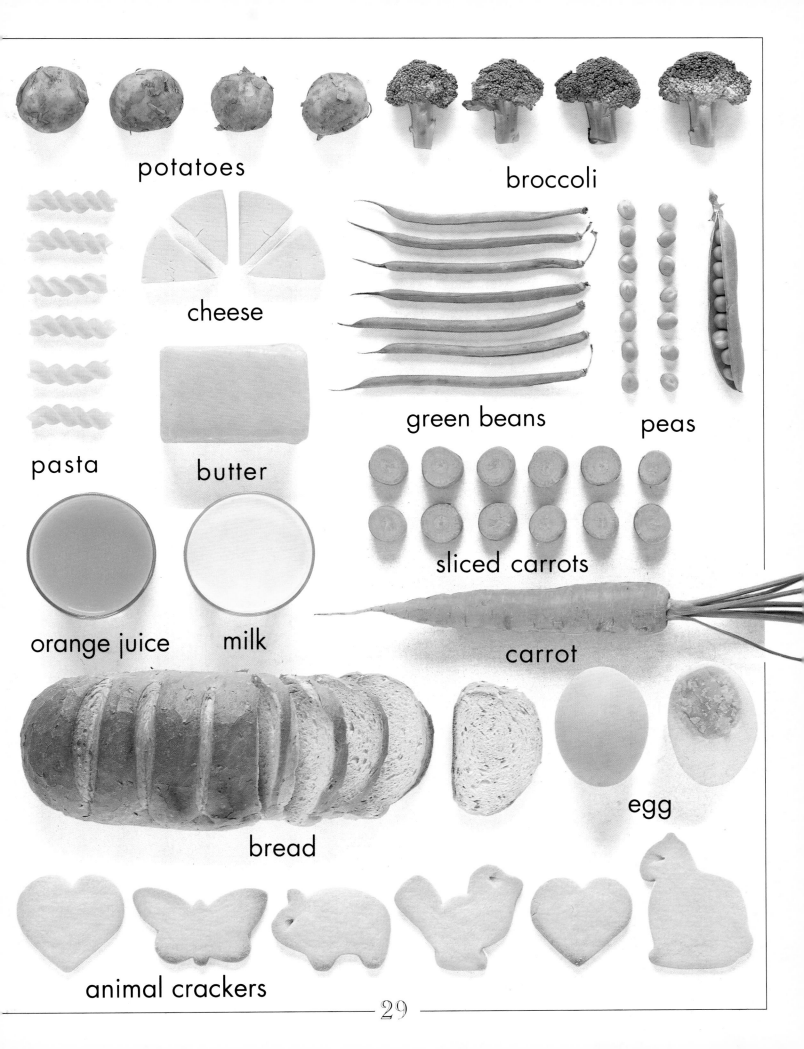

potatoes

broccoli

cheese

pasta

butter

green beans

peas

sliced carrots

orange juice

milk

carrot

bread

egg

animal crackers

29

In the Garden

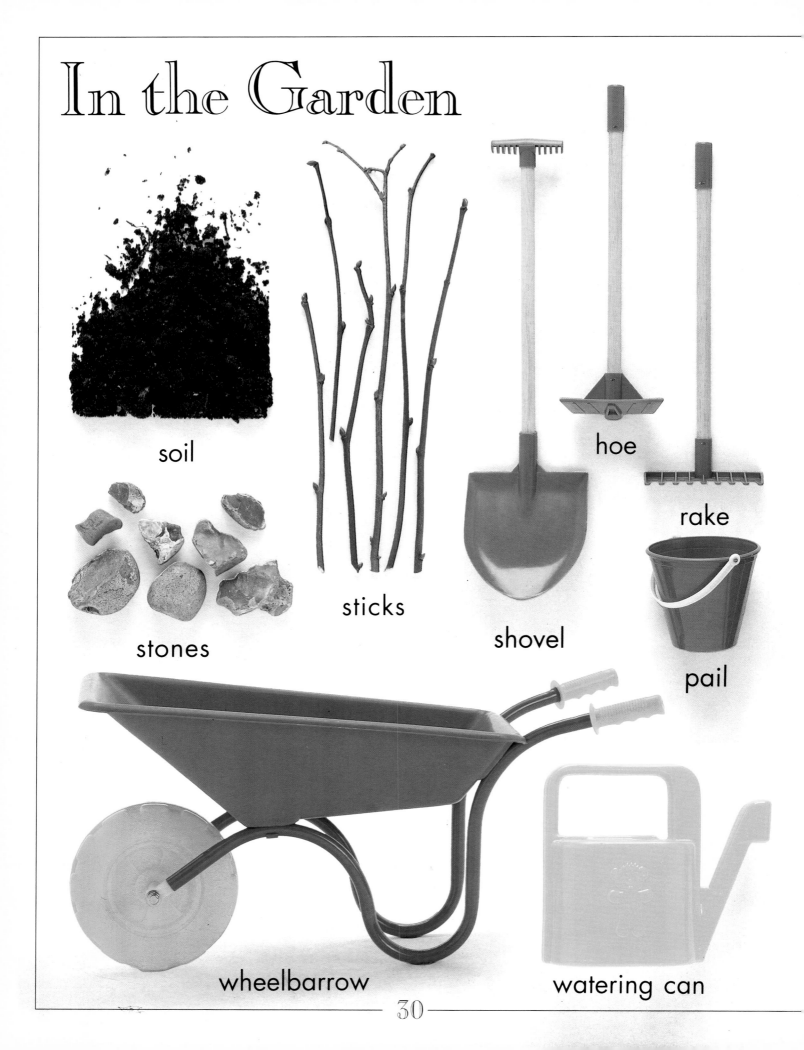

soil

sticks

hoe

rake

stones

shovel

pail

wheelbarrow

watering can

leaves

snail

flowers

plants

flowerpots

Sand Play

The babies are in the sandbox.

teddy bear
mold

ball

pail

umbrella

pail

shovel

pails

shovel

cups

Bath Time

soap dish

soaps

safety pins

bubble bath

towels

sponges

cotton balls

shampoo

cups

rubber duckies

sailboat

nailbrushes

toothpaste

toothbrushes

plug

tugboats   comb   hairbrushes

bath   activity   bar

talcum
powder

cotton swabs

In the Bath

The baby is in the bath.
The bath is full of toys.

Going to Bed

1. Baby is tired. It is bedtime.

2. She takes off her shoes.

3. She pulls off her socks.

7. Now baby is in her sleep suit.

8. She is sleepy and rubs her eyes.

9. Time for a quick drink.

4. Baby takes off her dress.

5. Off comes her undershirt.

6. And on comes a clean diaper.

10. Good night!

Counting

1 one

2 two

3 three

4 four

5 five

6 six

7 seven

8 eight

9 nine

10 ten